IRON MAN

AN ORIGIN STORY

Bath • New York • Cologne • Melbourne • Delhi
Hong Kong • Shenzhen • Singapore • Amsterdam

This edition published by Parragon Books Ltd in 2015

Parragon Books Ltd
Chartist House
15–17 Trim Street
Bath BA1 1HA, UK
www.parragon.com

ISBN 978-1-4723-8172-9

Printed in China

This is Tony Stark.

Tony is usually a regular guy like
you or me – but with a lot more money.

When Tony puts on his special armour,
he becomes more powerful than most people.
He even calls himself a different name.

When he puts his armour on, Tony is ...

... THE INVINCIBLE IRON MAN!

But Tony wasn't born a Super Hero.

He hasn't always fought to protect people.

But with villains on the loose such as Titanium Man and Iron Monger, who both use Tony's technology for their own evil purposes ...

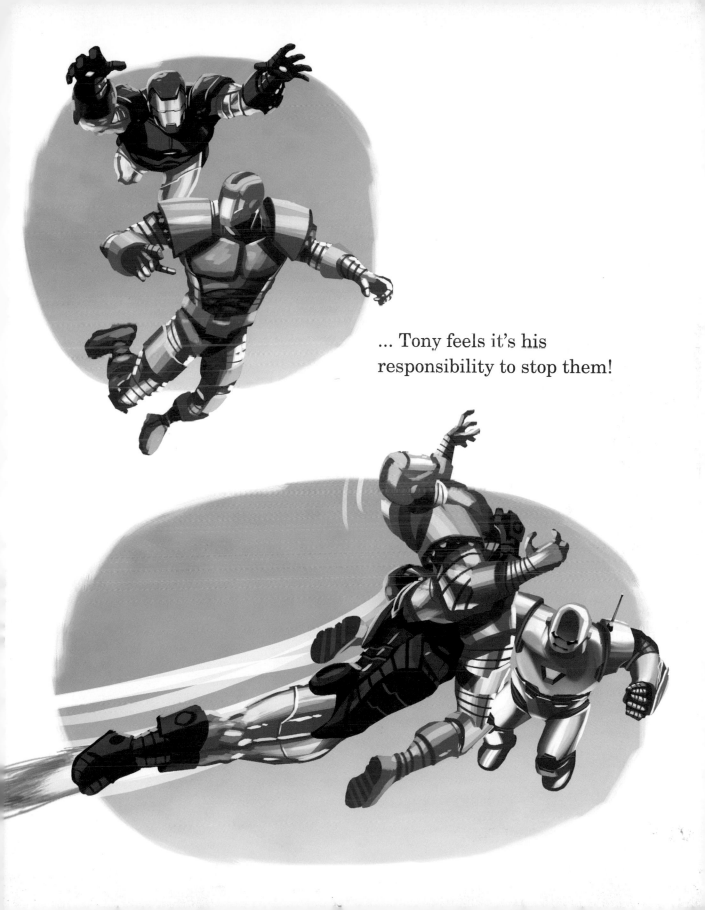

... Tony feels it's his responsibility to stop them!

Tony didn't always get the job done this easily.

Or this well.

Tony's armour wasn't always so sleek.

In fact, when he first became Iron Man,
Tony's armour didn't even shine!

But if you really want to know how Iron Man was born, we need to start with the man behind the mask. We need to start with Tony.

Tony had so much money that
he could go anywhere he wanted.

He loved to have fun.

And he loved the finer things in life.

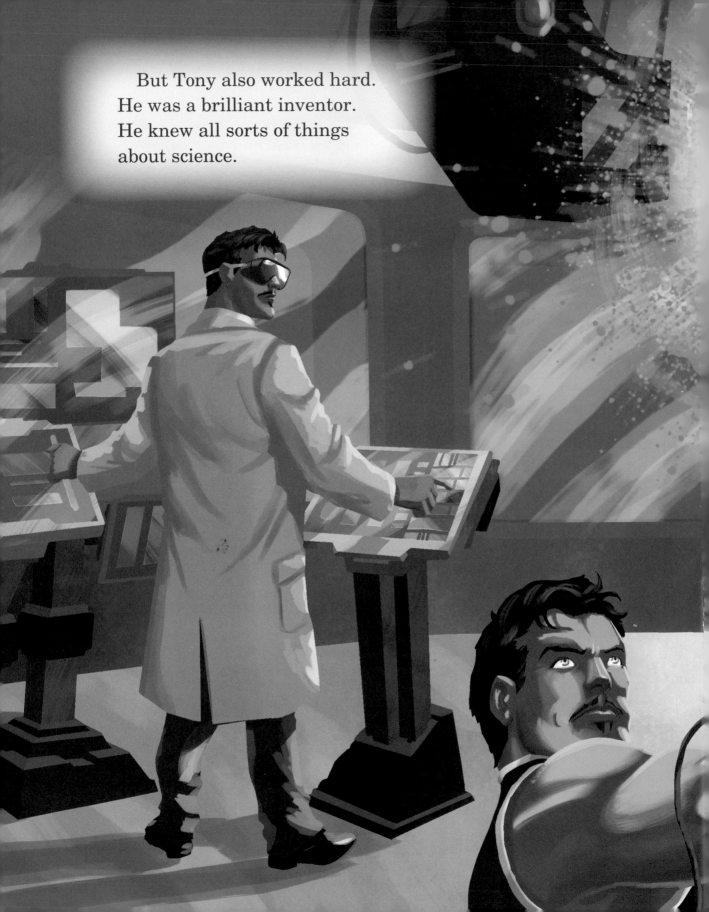

But Tony also worked hard.
He was a brilliant inventor.
He knew all sorts of things
about science.

He loved to work with magnetic fields. Using them, he created a powerful energy force that he called repulsor technology.

The military was interested in Tony's work. In fact, it was in a secret army lab that Tony's life was changed forever.

An enemy army had attacked and Tony was badly hurt!

Since Tony was famous, he was recognized right away.
The enemy knew all about his inventions.

They tossed him in a prison room filled with electronic and mechanical equipment. They wanted him to create a mighty weapon for them.

To make things worse, before the enemy left the tiny cell, they told Tony that his heart had been hurt in the blast. He did not have much longer to live.

Tony soon found he was not alone in the cell.
The enemy had captured another famous scientist
– Professor Yinsen. The enemy wanted the two men
to work together on the great weapon.

But Professor Yinsen had other ideas –
he knew a way to keep Tony alive!

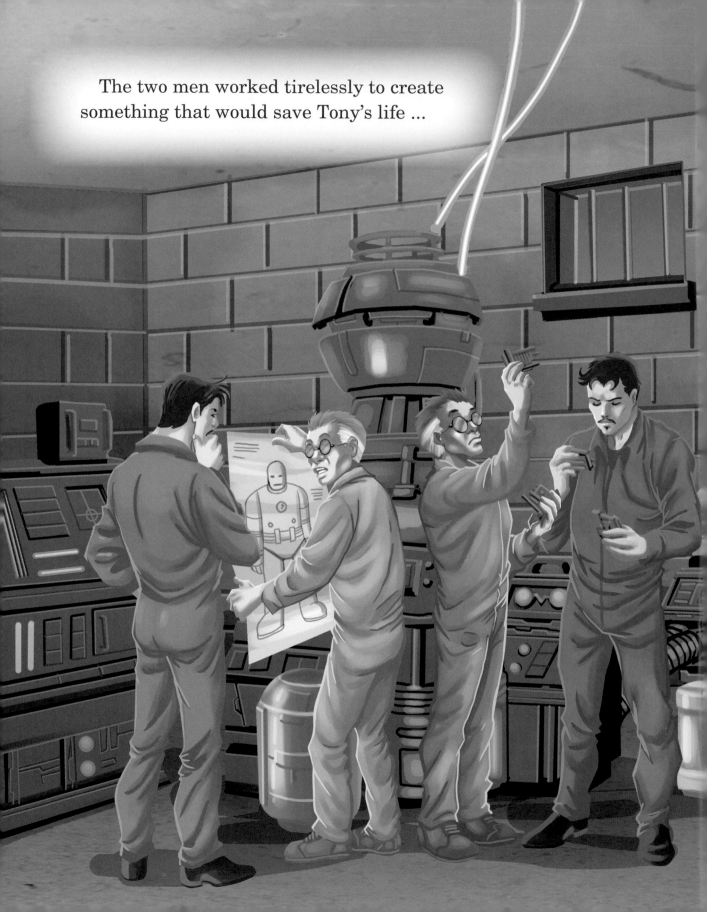

Finally, the men completed the device that Tony would need to wear from now on to keep his heart beating.

But that wasn't all they had created.

Using Tony's repulsors, they had built boots that could help a man fly!

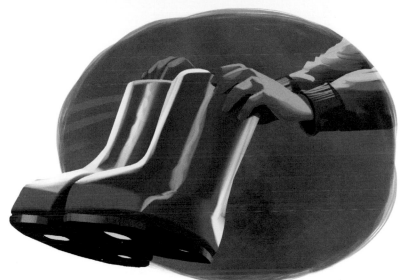

Gloves that could crush steel!

And a helmet that could protect a man from the most terrible blast!
Tony put on the armour ...

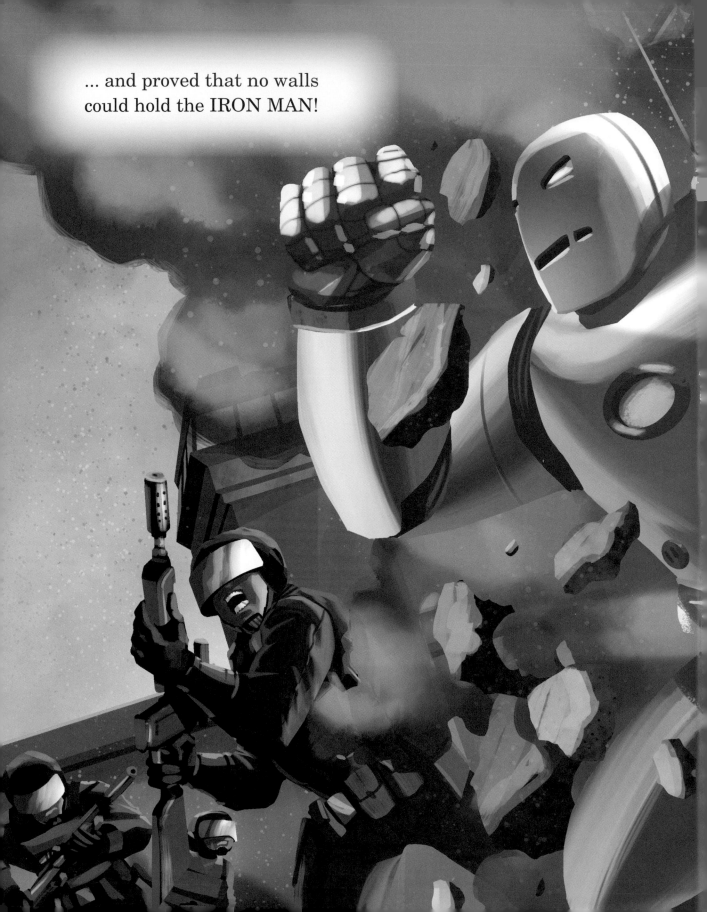

It wasn't long before the enemy realized ...

... they were fighting a losing battle!

Finally, Tony escaped from
the prison and flew back home.

But as soon as he got home, he realized
that he could now help where others couldn't.

Tony to the rescue!

He was strong, unstoppable – and frightening!

Maybe a little too frightening....

Tony had an idea.

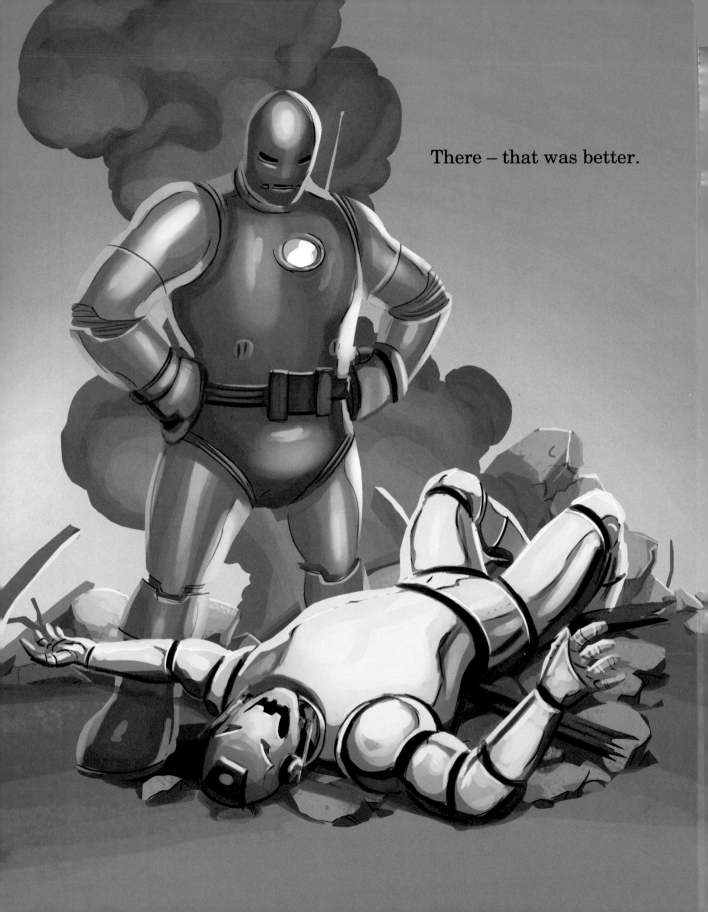

There – that was better.

Almost better.

Back to the drawing board!

Tony thought that Iron Man needed something as smooth and stylish as he was. He needed to create a lighter suit.

All he needed was for his chest plate to remain attached. Everything else could be changed.

Soon, Tony perfected his armour ...

And as Iron Man, Tony never stops fighting.

He protects people
at home ...

... and around
the world.

And when he's not fighting for justice as Iron Man ...

... Tony runs his company,
Stark Industries.

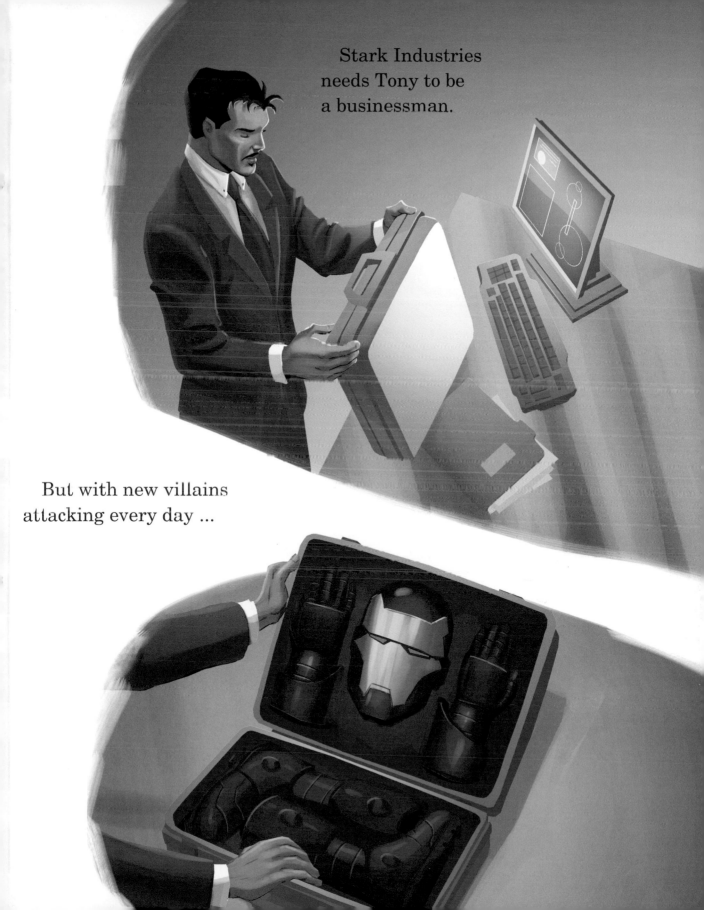

Stark Industries
needs Tony to be
a businessman.

But with new villains
attacking every day ...

... the world needs
Tony to be an Iron Man!